Open Slowly

Open Slowly

Dayle Furlong

TIGHTROPE BOOKS

2008

Tightrope Books
17 Greyton Crescent
Toronto, Ontario
Canada M6E 2G1
www.tightropebooks.com

Canada Council for the Arts / Conseil des Arts du Canada

ONTARIO ARTS COUNCIL
CONSEIL DES ARTS DE L'ONTARIO

torontdartsbouncil
An arm's length body of the City of Toronto

Editor: Shirarose Wilensky
Copy Editor: Myna Wallin
Cover Design: David Bigham
Typesetting: Carleton Wilson

Produced with the support of the Canada Council for the Arts, the Ontario Arts Council and the City of Toronto through the Toronto Arts Council.

Printed in Canada

LIBRARY AND ARCHIVES CANADA CATALOGUING IN PUBLICATION

Furlong, Dayle
Open slowly : poems / by Dayle Furlong.

ISBN 978-0-9783351-3-7

I. Title.

PS8611.U75064 2008 C811'.6 C2008-901596-7

For my sisters Karen & Jo-Anne

Contents

I

Impossible Permanence

She Seeks Beauty

She seeks beauty everywhere
foraging for flowers in fog
as the metallic din of machinery bordering
the park clangs and disturbs—she dislikes
comments we make about the weight of bulbs
all they have to do is sit, look pretty, and breathe
in truth, they're fibrous, sturdy, necessary for life.

She's culpable as any, flesh covers bone
like a clenched fist
taut in sections, ample in others
the weight of water and salt,
breath noxious

she tells us flowers deceive like a woman
warns us to watch out for the men hiding behind them

they cast shadows on sun
etch their place
on earth, bodies pyramids
of accomplishment.

While we sit pretty and still, necessary.

Impossible Permanence

Sweet spring with an aching afternoon sun
children whisper sugar-pop songs
of a love they know nothing of
but of this love they'll grow to know and it will
remind them of these afternoons:

when they were sweet, young, curious things
—aching grasses trembling to emerge.

Those loves, like these days, will forever
be the thing of memory

bristling to life at the suggestion of a song.

And we are left stupefied at recall:
emotions rise swiftly and we are young again
spinning, beaming, singing of lives we know nothing of

how our unknown future had always lain beneath like layers of
carelessly strewn early spring snow—an afterthought, a hiccup of
clouds that have talked too much—fancy dancing flakes seeking
impossible permanence.

Disappear

Little else matters

when I walk down this pretty street
and the green trees sweat a melon sweetness

while the moon hangs behind sullen clouds
—gasses gathered in a tumble
imprecise relations—
friendly bushes sashay like hips

all I want to do is pull them from feet-like roots
cup them in curled fingers the way I cupped you

but I must hang up these sentiments
old and unreturned.

For all I have
is this moment:
and it will disappear
as you did.

Bite the Wind

Trinity-Bellwoods Park on an early spring afternoon
the earth smells of clinging soil, desperate to thrive
my niece throws up her arms and tells me she loves nature
questions why we must cut so many trees to make paper.

She's quick for a seven-year-old, notions of revenge taut:
"If you cut trees for paper," she says,
"Paper will get you back and cut your fingers."

Got it all figured out, passive paper: sly, full of cunning slits
siphoning into gentle skin.

She tells me she wants to bite the wind, wrangle it,
throw it on the other side of the world, she's tired of
stray hair licking her face and choking her.

Instead we run, up and down the little hill, through the valleys
and briar-like bramble patches that crack and creak, dry as paper,
prickly as leaves.

Shannon Giggling

She giggles and it's river-like
eyes: skipping stones
an effulgence of light

arms: twig-like trawlers
meandering over a milky
current torso

nipping, tucking,
lapping at shores in warm ripples
and rivulets

legs: sediment, ginger bedrock
she aches a sweet refrain:
soprano giggles.

Flight, Freely

They shriek and cry as they twirl
on the merry-go-round
squeal as their thighs burn on the slide

soles flicking dirt
cotton straps dangle from shoulders
brushing past tiny hairs on arms.

Seagulls cry like children
—delight and hunger sound the same—
foragers both: one seeking a crumb, the other
a place to play.

The sea of children, mouths full of crumbs
falling in between toes—smelling of coconut oil
or vanilla ice cream, attracting gulls like flies.

Summer's children will play
tight-knit webs of friends
tangled on monkey bars
they swing, as in flight, freely.

A Prairie Storm

Driving in southern Manitoba
fields dominate either side of the highway—
a lustreless cement ribbon
that plows through the land
undeterred and unapologetic.

Flax: a shimmering violet, the colour inside
a dried and cracked oyster shell
glimmering and iridescent.

Sunflowers: a bolt of yellow silk, speckled with brown seeds
tawny leaves smoulder and curl as
waves of heat tremble above.

Wheat: fastidious and silent
beige limbs, slim and sturdy, emerge cleanly
from the tangle of muck and root beneath the dutiful display.

When the sun wanders off and the plum-coloured sky
rolls through, the sparked vein of lightning rips and tumbles like a
gambler's die: uncontrollable, haphazard, wily and wild
and we fear what will burn
from this electrical bet
between sky and earth.

For all their fluttering

moths land heavily
dark grey ink spots, murky and granite
in repose

the illumination they seek
an illusion

will their dance slacken
or will they continue to traipse floridly through time
big black signals of day
passing into night

will we be as desperate as those
insects hovering around the lamppost
lit by the invisible hand of the city
—the switch on auto—
fighting the darkness in these summer months

as we seek the nectar of a burnt and tired sun.

Opening Slowly

Autumn will come soon
and we'll live like lazy flies
swirling in the hot syrup
of Indian summer—an inverted tornado
plying us to the ground
weighty, listless.

Windows will be closed but a crack:
"Rapists won't enter slightly opened
entrances—they need garish slits
and wounded glass,"

he tells me as he exhales smoke
like a shadow from his ever-opening
fine-lined mouth: sucking prune-like
and territorial.

As he speaks, all I think of is you and
how I want to show up unannounced
crawl through your window
beg you to love me
through nakedness and entwined limbs

suck on your flesh as if it were dough
to help me rise up and above
this marrow, this vacuum of solitude
like a shadow on the pane of a
window—opening slowly.

Smoked Out

Autumn flies
land on feet
lazy and dry
no longer sprightly
as in spring—flight patterns:
dizzy, erratic, coy
their touch a tease.

Old men
on park benches rarely move—
their fly-wing skin
sags around necks
as they roll cigarettes tight-fisted
between rubbing palms

sitting still, inhaling thick sticks
that smell like wet leaves and cinnamon
smoking out all insects proclaiming:
"No fresh flesh here."

Eventually the flies swarm away
but not before some are caught
by a languid strike from a stray finger
like an old toad's tongue
licking them to death.

Flies

caught in a tangled
web, carefully stitched
between rusted pipes

in some long-forgotten boiler room
one in a nose dive, flight suspended,
others graceful—trapped in moments of pleasure
stuck fingers in warm honey

matted in a tangle as stray eyebrow hair
in hot-wax strips—pulled to reveal beauty
their wings raw, taut, stretched as if smiling
dancing on display.

City Sparrows

Raindrops like beads of oil
suspended on rubbery thin branches
bowed under the weight of drenched
autumn leaves: russet buttons of veined brocade.

Purple leaves like discarded grape skins
lie at our feet; when walked on
worms writhe out of soft shells.

The birds nestled between leaves
—swollen red breasts like berries—
patter along charcoal twigs
hungry under their cheerful chirps.

The city is suspended above
a creeping ivy grows up the side of the church
my mortal eyes, round and full,
can only see sheets and lines in the sky
ellipses and landscapes.

And the birds grin cheekily, chests heave silently
little swollen volcanoes for mouths gaping
chiding my limited view.

Romance Brief

Leaves lie in piles—
a blazing circus of decay.

Not so long ago they were
buds of spring that lay on
branches, ova to be
fertilized

romance brief—with clouds and rain
a summertime fling
heartbreak in autumn.

> *If they knew of the fall*
> *would they bother at all?*

I turn to you, feel you clutch
my hand—a rhythmic heartbeat—
our torsos cling to one another
on park benches like vines
watching leaves blow by:
dry, prickly edges scratch the earth
fingernails seeking permanence.

I'll raise my hand, rub
the apples of your cheeks
you remove memory from beneath nails—
past flesh under skin;
because I fill the
crevice and in our embrace
we are a trellis
a medley of coniferous promises.

Bare

A bare trunk, slim and shady
as a greyhound

blunt snout
sawed off by a bitter wind

branches poised on hind legs
racing towards a spring
that finishes last.

On another limb a parade
of chicken feet upturned—wrinkled
pointed claws on saggy, pimpled
wrinkled bark—
grasping and accusatory

leaves plucked
ready for slaughter.

The Ceremony

Rickety, bare branches stand like haughty witnesses
point grey, cruel fingers—condemning the ceremony.
This blizzard tosses them aside
breaks them if they are too obstinate.

First trickles, innocent fat flakes,
arrive like the unpinned strands of a winter bride's hair
flirtatious coils wrapping themselves around branches
slyly.

The sun shines in thick bands of golden light
through bursts of snow—confetti that announces
the smother that is to follow.

This blizzard thickens to make a veil
blocking our vision with gaseous, gathered clouds
flowing, swirling: blessed, sanctimonious robes.

We mistake this cocoon for safety
the stillness of the coffin-like lumps
hiding the ice beneath.

Diminutive Minuets

Snowflakes a tumbling minuet—
diminutive piano keys tinkling
mutely

the wind howls a cappella.

Blue Lips

Staring at the world in January
I see nothing but the mechanics
of the everyday

feet burn with the itch of cold
as streetcars break down, collide
while buses and trucks
amble by awash in
cement tones

we climb stairs covered in salt stains
like starchy spilt milk
—a trail of light to guide us home—
snow flicking like a glib comment
from heels too tired to make sentences

exhalations from tailpipes that look
like dirty throats
and the vapour that hangs around mouths
in puffs reminds me that life is still working
—shifting like grains of salt—
inhalations brief for a common
pause, those invisible moments that hang
around our blue lips while we suffer
what is natural and pray
to be released from the
whip of winter.

Respite

They'll force feed
you hunger

until your feet
can no longer
eat dirt
and the hustle
of listlessness

binds you and
makes you bleed
salt from pores so
sterile you'll
wonder about decay

it'll be all air
and no ice
they promise
from balconies poised
to hone perfection
I won't do this
you'll say
and ask for change
on your way out
the door.

Lazy Eye

Solemn puddles lie
adrift on sidewalks
too cracked to offer irrigation

unblinking eyes
icy eyelids melted
they'll sit and torment us
with their wide-eyed stare
warbling at the edges
ready to overflow

mud and dirt clouding
vision, tarnishing reflection

all I can see is this
melt on its way to spring
and wonder how did it
get here—and why won't it
be here tomorrow

like the faces I meet in the street—
the people in my life
mere puddles waiting to evaporate
right before my eyes.

The Thaw

It's still fairly icy but we are
outside anyway, desperate for patio season
cold weather no deterrent for Canadians
hell bent on spring

the chai latte is hot
and the cinnamon clumps
together at the bottom in cliques

lovers cheeks are sun-burnt,
clove when truly flushed
damp, musky.

I'll yell at the sun for
bull-fighting with clouds
demanding respite: a stable
sun elsewhere shining for now

while you laugh, sitting across
from me, my friend,
and I can see the youth in your eyes
and hear the thaw in your giggles.

II

Tonic & Brevity

Solos & Duets

jet zips up sky
choking blue silent
expulsions of air

fuming in puffs
warmth is exchanged
for something cool

sky blazing peach flesh
a bunched belly
cramping pinks through
clenched clouds

clouds, hungry teeth
gobbling up joy
with saliva-sized raindrops
mouldy teeth, unwashed,
spit on us

blossoms of sun emerge
between terrifying reds, bursting
flammatory violets

human eye roves, neck cranes,
we want to dance with it, but only
suffer its movements
an unwitting partner
caught in the folds
of cirrus' windswept dress
a cacophony of cackling clouds.

Tonic & Brevity

Alive, we have more tonic & brevity
than a circus parable will ever allow—so I cling
to it: this eternal promise, given when my mind couldn't
fathom an adulthood any less fabulous than what I had
dreamt of on bunk beds—hiding from the sharks below

    free from teeth and ache
    free from growing pains in knees
    and the shame of cheap sneakers.

I'd wear pretty dresses
and meet men from big cities

but you, my rural troubadour,
are the one in the end—the one who
loves me softly.

Past Flesh

My father carried me home on his back
from the pony rides at the community fair.

Every summer he smelt of coconut oil and he'd lie
in the sun until his back was the colour of a golden pecan—
skin puckering on either side of his indented spine.

I'd bury my face in the nape of his neck
snuggle into the warm, sweet-smelling flesh.

My mother buttoned my sweaters when the temperature changed
her hands, steaming and soapy, plump and round,
smelt tart and crisp from the green apple dish detergent.

Her wet fingers climbed clumsily up the row of buttons
slipping like insects on wet stones.

She'd pat my chin and tell me I was
the apple of her eye
and I'd cling to her—a nugget in the folds of her
soft, enveloping flesh.

Before a long day at school where neither back nor hand
could comfort or protect;
where they were hard as shells,
rotten as fermented fruit.

You Were Here

Leaves, giant tongues
veins plump—forked lightning bolts.

Precocious, he spat pop
and snot through his nose
—my childhood friend.

The delicate work of attachment:
stems, clotted with oxygen,
merge towards branch and trunk,
roots, bas-relief bruises buried in black earth.

He chased us, climbed trees in seconds
turned over rotting chipmunks to show
us the maggots.

Such quiet postures, complacent,
heavy with responsibility
delicate wrists strained.

Kissed me first, other girls second
walked me home through forests
in a town so rural, man-made
trails and dirt roads our proud efforts.

Here, trees know the taste of exhaust
slapped dirty from air too tired to clean
its bruised, dirty knees.

I want to walk in forests with him now
but he's married with kids, I hear,
and the tired tree outside my window does not hold his shiny face
or his quicksilver smile.

Experiments with the Living

…if you were to extort the present from me
fully, in its current condition,
what future could we imagine?
what would we pursue?

—surely not follow lost wishes
on airborne eyelashes or beg for the
incongruence of love—

yet somehow you'd hold my hand softly
during these same song wars and slay dragons
with wreaths of wildflowers
kind enough to choke
any fire-breather breathless

because with you I remember hours spent sitting on
swing sets as the breeze turned colder than
the ice cream ceaselessly licked
blushing our noses cherry—
melting fears

now inquiries are embargoes
disagreements dissent
and the eternal what
brings me to if…

Dizzy Mountain Precipice

On a dizzy mountain precipice I dangle
precarious between
here and now—
then and maybe

he floats by
a dandelion seed caught on a breeze

my heart, a fat cherub
clumsy hands pluck at the veins—

a choir of children
could not capture
the harmony of this
lost love.

I plant memory firmly
on this mountain
a flag.

Vanished

Hiking tame hills
we wander fresh-faced
fearless through mossy
valleys and weedy forest scrub.
Lonely old echoes
a few aching flies.

At Lake Superior we
hum "The Wreck of the
Edmund Fitzgerald" mockingly,
embarrassed. No old bones, no sunken
masts—a crumpled newspaper bobs on the
surface like a flapping gull's wing.

Smooth stones maul the shoreline
segments of a backbone
the water's ebb a puppy's tongue panting
in quick spasms.

Placards date sediment layers
warn of mercury levels while
a heron emerges
from the inky forest
—eggshell grey, blue
folded paper toy in flight—
casting shadows on a swollen lake.
Our dusty hands shield sun
we salute and watch her sail into seclusion.

Soon our brown bags hold only
crumbs, grease spots, and sandy grapes
we drive back to town
passing the white clapboard
near the rusted railroad track—
a roadhouse strip show haunt
boarded up, grim with decay.

We imagine dancers in flashy
blue boas, red kimonos, ashes falling in
between toes, singeing vinyl
stilettos. Cheap panties sagging
from elastic gone soft as fresh
pine sap, bleeding cotton threads
hanging like cobwebs.

The boys will laugh
and I'll wonder where they've gone,
why they've vanished.

Hooks

Friends from youth have fled:
travelling across the ocean
sitting on their knees—
not in prayer exactly
but humbled mountains.

Little fish on hooks
gulp and cry
worms will die
but you keep me dancing
on a line
not hanging exactly
but hoping for their return.

And with them carelessness, youth:
a hook from which
I couldn't wait to
escape—
yet struggled against
ripped my skin needlessly.

But the sun has set
the moon is full
—a cow's underbelly
heavy and pink—
so we'll sit together
and you can talk
of all that is sweet
and I'll dazzle you
to help me not think.

Say Uncle

I

Sitting on swings giggling
stuffing candy into each other's mouths

dragging toes tickling the sand
each grain falling over the other
like laughter
a curvy line left in the sand
a coy trail like a finger
cocked, come hither.

That must have been what he saw
invitations in the sand
when he gestured to his niece with one
finger—a signal to come
down to the basement.

Placing bunched fists
in his pockets
shoulders hunched
eagerness betrayed
by the froth on his
upper lip: desire glistening
like sugar.

I sat on the swing, puzzled,
staring at her clothes—
sky-blue baby-doll pajamas
fringed with lace—fluttering softly,
sheets wet with her pee
hanging limply on the line.

Under his thumb, she
pleaded, bribed, begged,
desperation choking her face cherry red
when I refused to go in the basement,
fear of spiders and fingers
keeping me above ground.

I got up from the swing, candy wrappers
falling in a trail from my lap, leaving
empty promises of sweetness behind.

II

He made many messes with her on mattresses
and was sent to prison where he lay
night after night on a single bed
—stiff as a backbone.

Both insect and spider; caught in a web
of his own making: not soft,
glistening in the sunlight, full of the hazy promises
of youth, but steel gray
and severe.

Fifteen years later, twenty-years old
living in the city, thinking rural swing sets
and basements far behind,
I saw him again.

He sat on a barstool
beer foam on his upper lip, shoulders
limp, skin like unmilked cornflakes,
hissing at sexy women floating by.

I gulped my drink
abandoned my friends
ran home to fish out old photos
of her: fear says *Uncle*
when I see happiness streaming from
her eyes, even then, even though
spiders and fingers lurked
in the basement.

Park Study

I

Two men with linked forearms
—pale peach and mahogany skins entwined—
walk slowly through the park

the supported man stops, the younger one cajoles,
tugs on his arm; the old one
can't see, but can smell, the city sewer hole underfoot

he steps on concrete and collides with stone, body inert
the shuffling one tries another tactic
pushes him from behind
up the hill, little engines.

II

Two girls wiggle as if improperly assembled
flesh a lubricant for bewildered bones
hips suffer cigarettes and glamour

friends-to-the-end, one seeks approval
the other doles it greedily

they meet a boy, buy confidence and
good times and
push themselves up
high over hills.

Two Graces

The older woman's neck gathers in rolls
a thin layer of birch bark, peeling,
she'll hold it high to keep it taut.

The young one's jugular thickens when she speaks
full of passion and conviction
she dangles grapes from her hand in bunches
holds a popsicle stick, sucks on the last piece of ice.

There are moments when the older woman's confidence
flattens against her skull
like wet tissue
deodorant stains like dry onion skins cling
to the mid-section of her blouse:
she wears hurry and fear on her waist.

The young woman's legs are like plump aloe vera stalks:
fibrous, sturdy, yet soft
her ankles and palms turn outward slightly
when surprised: she's not yet grounded in practiced grace
and still bristles when angered.

Sisters

lie twisted in white sheets
like sweet pastries
arms entangled
legs curled under

matted foreheads damp
powdery baby sweat curling
their hair

every year they rise
emerge from the heat of
blanket and bed

and we bake, dance, and sing

these baby girls who mean
all but
everything.

In the Hummingbird Garden

We sit surrounded by a
handful of fluttering
hummingbirds

raspberry red, spearmint green, quandong blue

their pointy beaks pierce
each other's feathers
fierceness disguised by great beauty:
as they compete for sips of
sugar water.

The wicker chairs bristle
glasses of tart iced tea
sit before us and we sip slowly
our bare feet resting on warm sand
the forest overhead a shelter of harmonious green

while we pick at each other
mercilessly
jealous of each other's plumes and
affectations.

In the Butterfly Garden

I sit on a stone bench
the spring green mould resembles
the colour inside a cracked pistachio shell.

Tropical plants a drapery of
lazy, fat-lipped leaves
an electric blue butterfly lands
on a yawning pink flower
lactating nectar.

Her almond eyes are soft
her antennae a knotted bauble
of wiry filaments.

Her dainty limbs, busy and purposeful
she fusses then flutters her wings like a hand-held fan.

My heart, nestled among bone,
pulses, busy and purposeful
yet it flutters as I marvel at how such a tiny creature
can move another
as I sit and watch and
wait for these floods of feelings
on a mouldy stone bench.

Solid Leda

Frowning fish lips
suckle lichen
at her concrete toes
nibble human skin
flakes from fingers
tossing coins

a water basin drips
cemented to her rusted palms
splashes at the stone
base, startling lethargic
turtles

she's an abdicated
queen claiming
her quiet throne
setting roots in stone.

The Madonna of Monteverde

The children outside the church
have flat bellies, skinned knees
and machetes.

The black dog is hungry
puppies like lumps of coal
rest on their mother's paws
pestering flies as fat as their tails
trickle through their thick coats.

The Madonna has brown hair, blue eyes,
and pink, sharp lips—she resembles a picture of my mother
from the sixties—

she smiles as I give alms.

Coins fall from my fingers freely
fatten the silk collection satchel
until it droops like a full belly.

Monteverde—
filled with the steamy breath of a moody god
threatens with molten rock and
stinging hot springs:
clues to its inching displeasure.

Secrets

One man drops her off, another will join her
at the loud Portuguese café on Dundas West.

Raindrops heavy; thick secrets
I can't hear through the glass
or above her pretty, manicured dialect.

She's thin, clipped, precise
he enters: large, clumsy, drooping glasses
unraveling sweaters and fumbling manners
her tiny hands dance diamonds.

She orders for him, she knows what he likes
fat, dusty bread with cheese lolling like tongues
tattling—lopsided, melting in mid-sentence.

She tugs at the napkins, gives him one first
wraps her sandwich in paper before eating
he wipes his fingers on his knees, taps his feet.

They relax and eat contentedly. He looks at me,
his eyes flicker. She pulls him back with a glance
she's his for this brief moment, the length of this rainfall, this small
brunch.

Scattered

The plump heads of roses
chopped from their stems
lie at the feet of

alabaster angels

in a small mud puddle
outside the Portuguese church

a consecration

I can see my face floating above the petals
a ripple distorts the image

I am limbless.

A single pink rose

wrapped in plastic
abandoned at a busy café

each petal filled with palm-like lines
this vein for luck, this for future, marriage, wealth
soon the plump leaves will thirst
they'll stop pulsing water through the crooked pathways
of this sweetheart rose.

She sits before the flower and longs to reach out for it
pull it from plastic; drop her nose in its head and drink.

She practices smiling to herself
and paints her lips pink
she'll carry that smile until the skin wrinkles
small fine lines fall crooked and slack:
withered petals.

Lovers hunched

over sixty red roses
for her thirtieth birthday

his chest, exhales in a soft slump
hands bent at wrists
curled languidly
as he sits at her feet

her hands, fussing protectively
with the heads of the roses
arranging them like
chicks in a nest
scent like exquisite leather
dusted with cocoa.

III

Litany of Desire

Fresh Fruit

Sliced cantaloupe, skin a scalp
peach flesh brains

I must be out of mine
to have signed up for this

a baby who suckles

wipes juicy fingers on my white
cotton shirt, breasts bare
her little fingers pull

and she'll suck them roseate down to the core
this little seedling driving me crazy with dependence

sliced minds throw out seeds
the juice drowns fingers clean.

Own Hands

Tired of gazing down this self-same spot
the end of a pen

the world at my fingertips
ceases to excite, becomes
these words written: action over

they are done, deeds in and of themselves
goals, aspirations, manifestos—sit and whine

beg to be walked, fed, groomed
anything to wipe the ink from their faces

to widen girth and swallow the world whole
but all they have is me
hunched over, head in palms
bleeding elsewhere.

Wood & Nails

Your skin, creamy and translucent
your nose, long
and classic
full, red lips
stubby fingers, the only clue to

the work you do with wood & nails:
brings you endless blisters, your fingernails
mimic the ragged edges of the lumber
raw with sawdust and sandy, chipped corners.

The work you do with your hands:
trace circles on my body
chisel wood with tiny metal tools
rub thin edges with your blackened thumbs
brush my cheeks with the backside of your palm.

On your salary we'll never have a large house
you tell me you'll build me one
with your own hands and you
squeeze my thighs and hover over me, an arched
roof.

Bound

Lovers tumble
tangle in a knot
limbs like Picasso

encircling light
eyes flashing, hair flying
openings new, whole: unique.

mouths agape, wonder
a new excuse
to sit stupefied

content, without guile
as the ache of embrace
dissolves like sugar; flits through
fingertips like spilt powder

we sigh and know what's
important and true
not a skewered sense of truth—
the one used to manipulate
thoughts and make laws

but truth that is seen
sporadically, precariously by some—
like light or a brushstroke in a
spliced painting—all angles and soft
refraction: crevices deep, filled with
rubbed colour, blushing at the edges
tumbling into endless caresses
of loose ends.

Litany of Desire

My lips shed skin
in crisps
if only to love you
abrasively

bites on your neck
little tears on your chin

you will enjoy me as
blessed and savage
as I tumble head first into you

you'll teach me how to use an ellipsis
so that nothing is left out
or unsaid between us—

and the muses trumpet in my ear
about the state of our involvement
deft cleft notes of knowledge
they deliver; more murky and inky
than instinct

and my lips will stumble in sorrow
at your soft web of cynicism
and I'll hide, a Persephone in her
own underworld, and mourn your
satiation.

Entangled

I lie like a minnow
let you gulp me in
expel me at high tide.

A trawler you are: everything in your wake

even those you kiss to sleep
as you pull, nip, and tug
the bottom of oceans.

You remain—entangled
in my heart like seaweed
causing my lips to frown
a gaping fish.

Jester

Your words are whispered—
from lack of tumult.

I rear around, swivel my neck
to see what it is that makes you
sing morbid—so often and so languid.

"So precious is our time," you say
and I want to refute, cry blame, cause pain
but can only whisper muted screams to engage the ones
who destroy.

Underneath this blue canopy
we drink, dance, sing, and grumble dryly—
because, my dear fellow, what are you, the
court jester, if not our deepest desire
to grow up and capture
the villains?

dirty feet jazz beat

last night's
lipstick stain
sits on my lips

rubs faint kisses on
my coffee cup
blushes pink my
fingertips
as I brush strands
of loose hair
free from my face.

I wandered last night
meeting mismatched eyes
that know as well as I do
that there's no one to go home to
save a roommate with closed doors,
candlelight, and soft whispers
that stop when the door
opens announcing your arrival

but I beat on—
find acid jazz clubs
fizzy drinks
mark beauty on my face
only to dangle boys
coyly from painted nails
and watch the dance full of wonder.

This Relentless Pursuit

The air is wretched and solemn
dirt: its own echo, reminders of pain,
shallow slivers—simple to iodize and sanctify.

I assent quietly—drink you in with proverbs
drawing attention to ethics and morality—
no noose around your neck—as you betray
sullen secrets.

Vertigo is your idea of success:
climb to great heights only to be pulled down
by buffoons blowing milk through noses.

I dream of a one-room apartment with fewer
roaches and a working clock radio
so I ingratiate myself to those holy enough to help
and wonder when did "business" become what it is
... and why do I still seek beauty
when those around me count pennies and favours
like buoys and demand
payment for help rendered?

I'll never remember how dark man can be: rapes,
trite murders, ambivalent betrayals—I toss them off like
gravel underfoot
because of this relentless pursuit of what's worth
being alive for—waiting around to see that
thing called beauty.

So, We

Someday there will be
new rhythms—beats unheard
equations born anew.

But when you leave, the click of the lock
makes me ache so
that I'll stare out the window at shadows
falling across latticework (never-ending, lopsided rows of sticks: a
precise relationship defined by a bead of air
trapped in a plastic tube; balance achieved).

And I'll turn up the Cuban jazz-count rhythm
so that the moment is bearable because
the tear of detachment
leaves me lopsided.

Even though I know that the work
of experience—like trekking to the theatre
or travelling: the effort of ticket sales, transportation,
the obligatory gestures and fumbling manners
of social display—will be worth it
and I'll hear a new rhythm and
it'll evolve somehow
into the next shadow of geometry.

Road Signs

In your eyes
the intermittent closure
of sad rain—

roads will close
and detours offer
themselves freshly

—but you'll keep crying
for the cloud
that caused such
electricity

even though his lightning
was a venomous, snake-tongue spit
and his thunder, bullying rams
locked inside white, slapping clouds

but he made you feel
soft and pink
not blue or grey as
sleeping asphalt.

So you'll continue
on this route
until the pavement dries
and the potholes are filled in.

Bruise

Her eyes a blue stroke
deeper than any shadow

a bruise left sudden
by too many tears
—a smear, a ripped cloud

her earnest innocence
a vaporous burr hanging
in the air ready to cling
like dripping ice

to anyone who loves her
anyone who needs her

ephemeral shades of sympathy
hide the blur of brilliance
yet how fresh she is: happy, hopeful
the torment worse in her mind.

She is loved, for the first time
she notices.

Acknowledgements

Thanks to everyone at Tightrope Books: Stacey May Fowles, Halli Villegas, Myna Wallin, and my amazing editor Shirarose Wilensky.

Thanks to Sumach Press, the editorial board of *Descant* magazine, for the Ontario Arts Council Writers' Reserve grant. Thanks also to *Taddle Creek*, *fhole* magazine, and *The Voice* magazine for publishing early drafts of these poems.

Thanks to the women of the writing salon for reading my work and offering suggestions.

Thanks to the following individuals who supported my writing process: Jane Dingle, Rebecca Hynes, Elena Hynes, Margaret Genovese, Eric Ojala, Karen Ennis, Phlip Arima, David Cooper, Shannon Cameron, Elizabeth Birss, Mark McKinney, Asher Mercer, Andrea Cowen, Robert Tang-Wai, and Marlene Mawhinney.

Thanks to my wonderful family Cynthia, Joe, Karen, Jo-Anne, Mary, and Sarah-Beth for the constant inspiration and love.